The Village that

By Sangeeta Mulay

Dedicated to all those who love humour and Science

First published in 2017 by Groggy Eyes Publishers

Cover by Mentol

Contents

Preface

In a tiny little village in India called Rampur, long before the time of smartphones, Wi-Fi, computers, and other electronic gadgets:

Chapter One

Tong! Tong! Tong! The holy Baba clanged the bell with all his might. Rambhau got up and stepped forward.

"My cows keep running away from me. They never come back. This is the fifth cow that I have lost this year, and I cannot afford to lose anymore. Please tell me a solution, Baba!" Rambhau said, with arms folded, bowing respectfully.

The Holy Baba stroked his podgy chin. Paunchy and bald, the Baba was always attired like the holy sadhus of yore.

"Hmm," he said. "It is very simple. Get up at dawn and perform three somersaults in quick succession every day. You will never lose another cow".

Rambhau gaped. He gulped.

"Err-somersaults?" said Rambhau, looking at his wide girth. Is there anything easier that I can do?"

"I'm afraid not. Next," thundered Baba. Rambhau stepped back after paying his respects to the

Baba, wondering how he was going to manage three quick somersaults in succession every single day.

Kala stepped forward. Dressed in a simple green sari, she had smeared red colour all over her forehead. Baba had suggested that this would bring her good luck and yet, here she was with her problem.

"I need a cure for my daughter. I do not know what has got into her, but she has taken into her head that she wants to become a teacher when she grows up. Raise babies, I told her. What good will becoming a teacher do? But she remains adamant".

"You are right to come to me," Baba said. We cannot have women working outside our homes. Housework, cooking, cleaning, raising children are what women are good for, and they should stick to doing that. They should not be getting ideas beyond that because that would cause chaos. Do not worry.

4

We will never allow your daughter to become a teacher in this village. We have plenty of capable lads for taking up that post. Just inform your daughter that she will never be able to become a teacher in this village".

The other villagers nodded with satisfaction. Baba always provided the right solution. Kala thanked the Baba with a somewhat forlorn look on her face.

Tong! Tong! Tong! It was now the turn of Keshavnath. He stepped forward.

"My donkey has broken her leg. I need her to carry wood every single day. I cannot afford to buy another one", he said.

The Holy Baba gave a loud burp. He rubbed his stomach contentedly.

"Why don't you wait for your donkey's leg to become better?" he asked Keshavnath.

"Oh, Baba. I cannot afford to wait. Think of all the money that I will lose in the meantime. That is why I have come to you. Please do not send me back without a solution".

"Hmmm. The solution is simple. Pluck out three grey hairs from your hairy head every alternate day. Your donkey's leg will soon become better", said the Baba.

Keshavnath was pleased. Last year when he had suffered from a stomach ache, the Baba had asked him to chase his neighbour's hen at least twice a day. Keshavnath still had nightmares about that time. Plucking grey hairs from his hairy head would be easy in contrast. He had those in plenty.

Tong! Tong! Tong! Nagnath got up and stepped forward. Clearing his throat noisily and bowing respectfully with folded hands, he said, "My brother Haripal has been exhibiting some really strange symptoms lately. He has taken to composing poetry and refuses to work in the fields. Day after day, he sits outside the hut, going on and on about the moon and the stars and some nonsense about love." Nagnath had whispered the last few words. Talking about love was not something that Rampurkars were accustomed to.

"How long has this been going on for?" asked Baba stroking his podgy chin. He had the villagers hanging on to his every word.

"Almost a month," said Nagnath ashamedly.

"Sounds like a simple case of devil possession," said the Baba, looking almost bored now.

7

A gasp went through the crowd. Cases of devil possession were extremely rare in the village which is not to say that they did not happen.

"The devil will need to be exorcised. Every moonless night, make your brother dance around the fire after midnight. Hit him on the buttocks with a broom every five minutes. Ignore his screams. Remember that it is the devil that you are really hitting and not your brother. When the devil gets tired of being hit, he will leave your brother's body".

"Can we go and watch the devil in Haripal being hit?" asked Keshav, unmasked glee on his face.

"Of course, but please maintain crowd control," said the Baba. Rambhau retreated with folded hands dreaming of the day when poetry or the devil or whatever had possessed his brother would leave him in peace to work in the fields. The Baba got up. The weekly problem solving session was over.

I looked at Damya and giggled. These weekly problem-solving sessions were turning out to be too good to miss. Every week, all of us Rampurkars would collect under the old mango tree in the centre of the village. The holy Baba sat on a raised platform close to the tree trunk and all of us sit around him on our bottoms. Looking at the faces of the villagers after the Baba comes up with a solution has become one of our favourite activities.

I wouldn't call Damya my best friend but let us just say that he is useful to have around. When I wanted to observe ants closely, hoping to learn something from them, it was Damya who helped me collect over fifty black ants. We kept them under a coconut shell, and I would allow them to run all over

9

my palms while observing their antics. I kept a few granules of sugar a few feet away from them to observe whether they would be able to sniff out the sugar granules. They could, and they did. Very soon I had a stream of ants going to-and-fro. I was thinking of building an entire army of black ants. Very interesting creatures, these ants!

Then there was the time when I wanted to plant a dead rat in the ground, wanting to see whether it would sprout leaves and it had been Damya who had helped find a dead rat for me. I told you that he was useful. The dead rat is still buried under the ground. I water it every day and closely observe the location where it lays buried. If dead seeds can grow into plants, then why can't dead rats? Damya had laughed at me. Of course, the rat is not going to sprout leaves, he had said. But why? I had asked. He had no answer to that.

Since the past week, I have been busy feeding some rice to the plants at night to make the plants fatter. Just imagine, how happy the village would be with fat plants. I overheard Mohan's Amma telling Mohan that he had become fat because of all the rice that he had been eating. If Mohan can become fat by eating a lot of rice, then why can't plants? Let us see what happens.

All these questions and ideas buzz around in my head all day long. Amma and Bapu do not have the answers to any of my questions. In fact, Amma gets really exasperated with my questions sometimes. I had told her in detail about the dead rat that I had planted. She had given me a long-lasting worried look. I heard her bringing up the dead rat with Bapu that night when I was pretending to be asleep.

"Should we ask the holy Baba for a solution? Something to make her a little less restless?" I heard her say.

They wanted to make me a little less restless. Quieten me down a little. Curb my numerous activities, ideas, and questions. Make me obey. Make me problem free. It was not going to happen.

I heard Bapu telling Amma that he would talk to Doctor Sahab about me.

Yes, our village also has a wishy-washy Doctor Sahab. Doctor Sahab had once explained to me that his role was to cure sick people. However, I see most sick people going to the holy Baba to get cured instead of going to Doctor Sahab. Baba takes one look at the sick person and - ta-da - he has the solution ready. Baba either tells them to burp thrice or to fart twice or to squat nine times to solve their problem. It is quick and

easy. Doctor Sahab's methods are too time consuming.
He has also been known to stick needles in your skin
which I find totally absurd. What good will that do?
Some Rampurkars do go to Doctor Sahab, but the
Baba does not like it. And everyone obeys the Baba in
this village. Doctor Sahab is too timid to do anything
about it.

I heard Keshavnath tell Bapu yesterday that
this village remains peaceful and happy only because
of the holy Baba. Only last month, Baba had scared all
of us out of our wits by telling us that there is an evil
eye lurking around in the village. If the evil eye looked
at you then – whoosh – you were gone. Some great
misfortune would come your way. Everybody was
terrified. I went around trying to find the evil eye in
remote corners of the village. Damya who was always
up for such adventures joined me. It was our intention
to try and spot the evil eye and then to squat it like a

mosquito before it had time to look at us in the eye.

We tried hard but could not find it. When Amma heard that I was going around the village trying to find the evil eye, she gave me another one of her looks – full of worry and sadness this time. It almost made me want to remain trouble free. Almost.

Eventually, all the villagers begged the Baba for a solution to the problem of the evil eye.

"The entire village should do a headstand at exactly four o' clock in the afternoon. They should stand on their heads for at least one full minute otherwise this will not work," was the Baba's advice.

So, for months together at four o' clock, all of us, the young and the old, would scramble to stand on our heads. Damya and I would go into a fit of giggles on looking at the futile efforts of the villagers to stand on their heads without toppling over. We kept toppling over ourselves. Amma, who just couldn't manage the headstand, gave me an angry look every time we laughed too loud. This was a serious matter (according to her); the evil eye could not be laughed at. However, it was too much for Damya and me to control and we continued to guffaw.

Finally, after a few months, the Baba told us that our headstands had paid off. The evil eye was gone. Everyone heaved a sigh of relief and went back to their work.

Bapu says that the holy Baba and the tall and portly Sarpanch of the Gram Panchayat are the two most powerful men in the village. Everyone is a little scared of them. The villagers shower the Baba and the Sarpanch with gifts which are often delicious things to eat. They believe that if we keep the Baba and the Sarpanch happy, then we too would be happy. I do not know whether we all have become happy because of showering gifts on the Baba and the Sarpanch. All I know is that the Baba and the Sarpanch are getting fatter, day by day.

Doctor Sahab told me once that he wasn't born in Rampur. He had studied in the adjoining village of Seetapur and only came to Rampur as an adult. He then went on to tell me a very curious thing. He told me that he had studied a subject called Science. Science! It was for the very first time that I heard the word. For some reason, I have never forgotten it. Unfortunately, I do not know what it means, and Doctor Sahab wasn't much help.

We are taught every subject in our school except for Science. Doctor Sahab told me that he is the only one in the village who has studied Science and even his knowledge is now getting a little rusty because of lack of use. He is too timid to do anything about it.

Bapu tells me that sometimes the Government of India forgets about tiny villages like ours. It is for this reason that it has forgotten to send a Science teacher to our village. This has been the case for years and years. No one knows anything about Science. Doctor Sahab had hinted that Sciences might just have the answers to some of my questions. That made me even more curious about Science. When I discussed this with Amma, she told me that she was a little fearful of Science because she did not know anything about it. Now isn't that a shame?

Chapter Two

"Dark, curly and unruly – your hair is just like you,"

Amma says each time that she oils my hair for me.

That is true – my hair is a lot like me because I cannot

control it. It chooses the direction that it wishes to

grow in and I cannot persuade it to change course. My

hair resembles the tangled roots of a weed that Damya and I had once plucked out from the ground. It is not really tangled, though it gives the impression of being so and is always clean (Amma picks out all the lice every Saturday) but it does look a mess.

Amma often tells me the story behind my name. When she first saw me, purple and wriggling soon after birth, she says that I looked exactly like a dark juicy Jambhul fruit and so she decided to name me Jambhula. Jambhuls became my favourite fruit after I heard that story. Damya and I love eating them, and we often go around with our purple tongues hanging out, trying to repulse people off.

I live in a small hut in the corner of the village. My hut gets a new look every season, so things are never boring. Bapu tries to make the roof as sturdy as possible during the monsoons, by piling up everything that he can think of on top of the hut to prevent the water from leaking in. During the summer, he tries to make the hut light and airy by removing almost everything that has been piled on top. We end up sleeping under the stars in the summers anyway because it is so cool and lovely outside.

The best thing about my hut is that it does not have a toilet *inside*. We go out in the fields early in the morning to poo. Amma gets up before sunrise so that she can poo in the darkness. I do not bother. I go to the fields when I need to, and if I catch anyone trying to peek, I will beat them till they change colour. The grass in the fields has been kept tall to prevent any peeking. Sometimes, it is a challenge, to find a clean, safe spot especially if several people have been having a feast the previous day. However, our poos mix in the soil in no time at all, so every day is a new beginning, so to speak. I simply love pooing in the wide, open fields and cannot understand how the city people manage to poo in dingy, closed rooms. In all my eleven years of life, I have never ever pooed inside a room and have even made a solemn proclamation that I will never ever do so. Most of the Rampurkars share my view. The thought of pooing in a closed room inside the house horrifies us all. We find it utterly and truly gross.

I come from the dark lot in the village. All my ancestors have had dark skin. We are lower, and the fair-skinned are higher. (I do not know what this means, but I have heard Bapu repeat this often so it must mean something). There is a belief among the villagers that the darkies are impure (this, despite me taking a bath in the river every single day and smelling like the fresh frangipani) and so we are not allowed to enter the main village temple. Some Rampurkars do not like to eat with us for this reason. Some fair-

21

skinned villagers do not like to touch us. We, the darkies, usually get to do the hard, "dirty" work like disposing of dead animals, cleaning the village, helping cremate the dead people, cutting stones and so on. You must have got the drift by now. Basically, it is work that no one else wants to do, and because the work we do involves dirt, we are considered impure. None of us object. We are used to the unwritten rules and have been following them for ages.

Radha belongs to the fair group, and I guess, you can say that we are friends despite that. If you really think about it, Radha and I are a lot similar. We are the same age, and she can fart as loud as I can (she does not hold farting competitions with Damya though like I do). We only differ in the colour of our skin, but that makes a lot of difference in this village.

There was a time in the past when darkies were not allowed to go to school. However, (thankfully) all that changed due to the efforts of some people whose names I cannot remember. Bapu had wearily tried to explain it all to me, but I found it all extremely confusing because most of the rules do not make any sense. They should let me make the rules for a change. That would be fun.

By the way, the colour of the poo of a darkie is the same as the colour of the poo of the fair skinned. I know because I investigated. I was curious to know whether poo colour changes according to the skin colour. For some reason, I thought that the poo of a fair skinned person must be a different colour but unfortunately, it comes in the same boring range of colours that my poo comes in. Yellows and dark browns and sometimes, though it is very rare, greens. When I reported my findings to Amma, she was livid.

23

She made me stand outside the hut for the entire afternoon and did not let me come in. When I asked her what I had done wrong, she just gave me a sad look and then gave me a brief hug. She is an expert at giving sad looks. I do not like her sad looks at all.

Damya is as dark as me, and he is treated differently too. He does not care either. Yesterday, he had given the fair Mohan a whack on his buttocks, and for that, Damya had got whacked by the Sarpanch. One whack begot another. It made me giggle as the picture of Damya giving that useless Mohan a whack, rose vivid and colourful in my imagination.

I went outside and saw Damya strolling nonchalantly chewing on a piece of sugar cane.

"Where did you get the sugar cane from Damya?" I asked him.

"E-r I found it," he said refusing to look at me.

"You stole it, didn't you?" I asked him.

"I will let you have a piece if you promise not to tell anyone," he said and so saying, he reached inside his raggedy shirt and stealthily showed me around 5-6 pieces of cut sugar cane pieces.

"Give me three pieces, and I will not breathe a word", I said. Damya reluctantly handed over the three pieces, and we strolled together. The juicy sugarcane felt soothing and very sweet in the hot afternoon sun. It managed to calm down the constant restless questions that were so often zooming around in my head.

"I heard that you were given a whacking by the Sarpanch," I asked Damya. Damya, who was as dark as coal darkened further when he heard my question.

"That idiotic Mohan! He thinks that he is too good to be true. I gave him one. A loud one that made all the dust fly off from his pants. The oaf!" he spat out his rage. "He created such a fuss and went and complained to his father. And I got beaten by the Sarpanch because of him. I am not going to forget this in a hurry", he continued.

"What are you going to do?" I asked him, all eager now. Damya did have some bright ideas at times, and I wanted to be a part of whatever scheme he was hatching. Damya looked at me for a second, debating in his mind whether he could trust me. There had been times in the past when I had let him down. The choice between telling on Damya and being whacked was not a difficult one to make, and I had told on him several times in the past to avoid being whacked. Damya, however, decided to trust me. He dropped his voice low and started to speak.

26

"You know the village temple – the one that we are not allowed to enter?"

"What are you going to do Damya?" I asked him, unable to contain my curiosity.

"Well, I have never ever set foot inside a temple because of all these rules. I think that the time has come to change all that. I have always wanted to see a temple from inside. I am going to break in at night and look." He said calmly.

I looked at him, shocked and speechless.

"You dare not," I finally managed to say.

"Santya and Ganya are going to join me too". He thought for a second. "You are welcome too", he finally said.

I was still in a state of shock. For all my not wanting to follow the rules, I knew that this was one of the most important ones. The entire village would beat our parents and us to a pulp, if they knew. Darkies could not break the unwritten rules. It would cause havoc. This was big! And it was exciting. It would be the most dangerous things that I had ever done. I thought of all the possibilities. We had to ensure that we were not found out – that was all. Once that was taken care of everything else would be easy. I had always wanted to see the interior of a temple. What would it look like?

"I'm in", I told Damya.

"I knew you would be", he said grinning.

Damya knew me too well. The temple was in a compound surrounded by barbed wire with a gate that was locked at night.

"The night of the full moon is when we have it planned for", he continued in a muffled voice. "You will have to sneak out of your house. The others and I will be waiting. We will have to sneak in through the barbed wire".

That would be no problem at all, I thought. All of us were a raggedy mix of skins and bones. The narrow gap would be no problem at all.

"No blabbering to anyone", said Damya. "Do not go around telling that Radha, for a start", he said.

"I am not stupid, Damya", I told him. There was no way that I was going to tell anyone. This was way too big for that. The thought of entering a temple for the first time in my life made me ignore my fears.

"I cannot wait, Damya", I said.

"Neither can I", he grinned.

Chapter Three

The holy Baba had gathered us all under the mango
tree. It wasn't the day of the regular weekly problem
solving session, but the Baba had told us that he had an
important announcement to make. He had already
eaten six laddus in the past few minutes that I was
watching him. Rampurkars believed that when Baba

was happy automatically, the Rampurkars would remain happy. I was thinking of ways to test this but had not come up with any ideas yet. The Baba looked happy, going by the loud belches that he had been uttering ever since feasting on the sugar-laden laddus.

"Rampurkars! As proof of my extraordinary powers, I have decided to perform an awesome miracle for you all." BURP!

There was an excited chatter and a few giggles. What was the Baba going to do?

"By the miraculous powers that have been bestowed on me, I will be walking on the embers –hot coal," he bellowed.

I gasped! People immediately began to bow down before him.

"Do not simply bow down. Get up. Get up", he said impatiently.

"If you want to benefit from this miracle then it is advisable for you to bring gifts to please the powers in the air. The powers are usually thrilled with sweet offerings. Err; the laddus that I was given today were very good. Nothing but happiness will be ensured by giving these sugar laden gifts".

The people, like sheep, nodded their heads in glee. How honoured they felt to be able to witness this miracle. They made up their minds to shower the Baba with even more laddus. It was only the fair skinned that could gift food to the Baba. The dark skinned had to help the Baba in other ways by doing odd jobs like repairing his chappals, cleaning up after him, washing his clothes, ensuring that he found a clean spot to do his poo and so on.

The date when the miracle would be performed was named. The time was specified.

On the appointed day, there was a buzz in the air. People started preparing laddus for the Baba. The Sarpanch went around on his rounds and was pleased with the pleasant aroma of ghee and sugar. The Gram Panchayat was pleased too because they had been promised a share of the laddus. All of them were looking forward to the sugary feast.

People started gathering under the mango tree with gifts in their hands. Some of them climbed trees to get a better view. In a few minutes, nearly the entire village had gathered. The Baba kept us all waiting. He knew that he was a very important person (VIP) and we waited and waited and then started to get a little impatient. The younger children were getting hungry. I was sent to fetch the Baba. The Baba was engaged in a deep discussion (intercepted with loud burps) with the Sarpanch. He kept us waiting for all of three hours. But who could complain against such a holy person?

He finally strode in and was soon the focus of all eyes.

"Eh Chiltya, go and get some coal" he ordered. Chiltya went to get the coal.

"Light it up", the Baba thundered.

Someone lit up the coal that was scattered all over the ground. The embers started to glow orange.

The Baba lifted his foot. A hairy leg could be glimpsed underneath his orange robe. A shiver of excitement went through the crowd. I suspect that the excitement was caused due to the miracle that the Baba was going to perform and not because of the hairy leg. He placed his foot on the glowing embers. There was a quick intake of breath in the crowd. The Baba then placed his other foot on the glowing embers. Quickly he walked the entire length of the burning coals on his bare feet.

There was a hush in the crowds. We simply could not believe our eyes. What a fascinating miracle the Baba had performed. He had actually walked on coal that was burning. How on earth was he able to do that? My mind was trying to work out the possibilities. I could see that the Baba was not in any kind of pain. The embers had not caused him any pain as was apparent. Nor had they caused any burns on his body. How then could this be done? It really was a miracle. Though I did not like the Baba too much, I could not but help feel really impressed with this feat of his.

The crowd rushed to him. They bowed and grovelled before him. They pleaded with him to accept their gifts. The Baba had come well prepared. He had bought a gigantic bag with him to keep all the laddus. He kept passing his tongue over his lips because the thought of eating all those sugary ghee laden laddus must have made his mouth water.

Our parents discussed this miracle for months afterward.

"How lucky we are to have the Baba within our midst" seemed to be the thought on everyone's minds. That night everyone in Rampur was content. We saw the Baba, Sarpanch and the rest of the Gram Panchayat sitting under the mango tree and eating until it was impossible to eat further. They must have spent a satisfied night replete with the sugary laddus. All the other Rampurkars were happy too. How lucky we were to have such a great man in our midst we thought to ourselves. We did not have even any inkling of doubt that we were being taken for a jolly ride by the great

Baba.

Chapter Four

On the night of the full moon, I was fidgety throughout the day. For the first time in my life, I did not go into one of my reveries by trying to work out problems in my head. In fact, I finished all my chores diligently.

All the plans were in place. We were to meet outside the temple and hide until we were ready to go in.

The plan was to sneak out in the middle of the night. I had managed to get myself into a state of extreme nervousness. Bapu was a deep sleeper, but Amma wasn't. What if she woke up and forbid me from going? That simply could not happen. I did not want to miss this great adventure. Furthermore, I was curious about the temple. What did the idols look like? What was their colour? What else was in there? How did it smell? Would it be dark inside? I would only know by going there myself.

I thought that Amma would never ever fall asleep that night! She kept sighing, tossing and turning, first this way and then the other. After what seemed like an extremely long time, she finally fell asleep, and I could hear her breathing steadily.

My one worry was that I would have to leave the door open after I slipped out and my parents would not be safe in the unlocked hut. What if a thief came along? There had been some stealing in the village in the past. Mostly goats or hens were stolen. However, who was I kidding? A thief would never choose our hut to steal from! We did not have any animals and hardly anything else worth stealing. What if a killer came along and killed everyone in the hut? There had been a murder in the village long before I was born. My mind had started to conjure up these nasty thoughts. But there was no turning back now. Everything will be all right, I assured myself. So, I took one final look at my sleeping parents and noiselessly tip-toed out of the hut.

It was a beautiful full-moon night. The entire village was asleep except Damya, Santya, Ganya and me, of course. I enjoyed making the unseen night animals scamper as I walked past. I made up my mind to take more of such nocturnal walks in the future. Everything was just so beautiful in the dark.

When I reached the temple, I was surprised to see that Damya had collected a whole gang of neighbourhood boys. There was Kalu, Girya, Chiltya and Tushya along with Santya and Ganya. None of them had been inside a temple before.

"Damya, you have collected the entire village, you idiot!" I hissed, feeling angry.

"All the darkies want to see the temple, and I do not see why not", said Damya with a giggle. There was some nervous laughter from the boys.

"Well, do not make any noise - I am in no mood to get beaten by the villagers", I said. In a way, it was probably a good thing that there were so many of us. I felt safer with such a crowd. They said that ghosts usually chose moonless nights for their excursions, but you never know; a ghost might just decide to take a walk on a full moon night and Damya and me alone, would hardly have been a match for a determined ghost. It was better to have the whole gang around.

The compound gate was locked, but all of us quickly scampered in through the barbed wire one by one. There was a lot of giggling, shoving and pushing and a lot of muffled laughter. I could not stop giggling. One by one, we all went noiselessly through the barbed wire. Damya nearly ripped his shorts while passing through and immediately there was a barrage of subdued laughter. We were now inside the temple compound. It was forbidden for us to be here and yet here we were - all of us darkies, breaking the rules to look at the interior of the temple. The feeling of anticipation was delicious. We could hardly wait now. Now that it was almost time to go in, all of us were silent. If anybody caught us now, then we would get much more than a mere whacking. Our families would probably be thrown out of the village. For a moment, I felt a pang but then I hardened myself. There was no turning back now. It was all going to be worth it.

The temple had a door, which was usually bolted. It would spoil all our plans if the temple priest decided to lock the door on this night of all the nights. Thankfully it was unlocked. Damya tried his best to slide the bolt open noiselessly, but it was a futile task. The bolt made a loud squeak each time Damya tried to move it. Each squeak of the bolt was followed by muffled giggles. Damya made a face at us, and we all held our breaths, hoping that no one heard. We waited for some time, and Damya tried to slide the bolt open again. It made another loud squeak. After seven such squeaks, we finally got the bolt open.

Damya flung the door open with a flourish. It rattled loudly against the wall. All of us pounced on Damya at once.

"Are you crazy Damya? Why are you making so much noise?"

The giggling started again, but all of us were a little nervous now. We did not want anything to go wrong. We were trying to be silent. A dog barked somewhere and then it was all quiet again. We entered, and I closed the door softly behind us.

We were standing inside the temple, and we were awestruck! The temple was clean and beautiful. It smelt of dried flowers, incense, and stale milk. The deities dignified and serene were at one end. The flowers that the villagers had bought in the morning were still placed in front of the idols. A small bowl of milk which had been used as an offering to the deities stood on one side. The fair skinned villagers often made offerings of food to the deities, and according to Radha, milk was the most popular offering. One of the idols was pink and gold, and the other was blue and gold. One was a female deity, and the other was male. Both had peaceful smiles on their faces. There was also a small money box placed in front of the idols where people could drop in coins as offerings if they wished. I saw Damya looking at the money box with a gleam in his eye. But the gleam vanished even as I was looking at him. Even Damya was not foolish enough to steal money. He went to the incense instead and started sniffing it greedily.

It was all just as I had imagined. We were quiet. I could not get enough of the temple and kept

46

looking around trying to take it all in. I wanted to ensure that I would remember the scene and would be able to summon it up in my memories whenever needed. We all knew that we would never be able to set a foot inside a temple again and we wanted to make the most of it. There was still some doubt in my mind as to whether God really existed but that did not stop me from enjoying the aura of the temple.

We spent nearly an hour inside the temple. Then, very reluctantly, we decided to go home. Damya carefully bolted the temple door, and we scampered out of the barbed wire. We were silent on the way back, each of us with our own thoughts. We were probably the first darkies in the world to set foot inside an Indian temple (unless, of course, wicked young darkies like us, had dared to do it before without anyone having a clue).

Chapter Five

It was the end of March, and the mango trees all over the village were heaving and panting with fresh, green mangoes. This was one of the reasons why I loved the spring (and summer). There was always so much to eat outdoors! There were green mangoes, which then ripened to irresistible juicy golden ones. There were

Amla trees, and I loved tasting the sweet and sour juice of the small Amlas. Jambhuls though are my favourite. I was named after the fruit after all. Damya and I had lots of fun eating numerous Jambhuls and then walking around with our purple tongues hanging out, trying to compare who had the brightest tongue.

On that lazy summer afternoon, I was perched high up on the deliciously sweet smelling branches of a mango tree. I had come well prepared and was carrying some salt in a small paper pouch. It was a muggy day, and the cool green branches were soothing with their calm shade. I plucked a raw mango and wiped it on my skirt. Opening the salt pouch, I dunked the mango in it and then prepared my taste buds for the onslaught of the rich sour taste. Taking my first bite made me scrunch up my face. It was very sour - in a very enjoyable way. I loved eating these raw and crunchy mangoes– white on the inside and dark green and hard on the outside.

I was so set on the task of relishing the raw mango and felt so peaceful and cool in the leafy branches, smelling the ripening mangoes and listening to the bird cries all around when something suddenly hit me on my leg. Glancing down, I wasn't very happy to see Damya appear with a huge smile on his face. It was a pebble that he had thrown that had caught me on my leg. I wanted to be left alone and was in no mood to chat to Damya. Before I could stop him, he had already started to climb the tree and had plucked a raw mango for himself.

"Can I borrow some of your salt, if you still have some left?" Damya asked.

Sighing, I handed over my salt pouch to Damya. Damya settled himself in the lower branches and started to hum a tune.

"Pipe down, Damya", I said, "Why are you always so loud?"

Damya then started to whistle tunelessly. I made an exclamation of annoyance, under my breath.

"I have just heard the most amazing news ever!" said Damya. "Ganya's aunt is a witch!" he said, dropping his voice to a wicked whisper.

"What nonsense are you prattling Damya?" Though I acted disinterested, I was very curious about Damya's latest story. Ghosts, witches and evil eyes fascinated me, and I always wanted to know more.

"Haven't you noticed her piercing green eyes? She is the only one with green eyes in the entire village. She hardly ever blinks!"

"So, she is a witch just because she has green eyes?" I asked, bursting into peals of laughter. "That is the silliest thing that I have ever heard in my entire life!" I tried to remember if Ganya's aunt had ever blinked at me and could not remember.

"She goes wandering off on moonless nights, to meet her friends on the outskirts of the village". Damya seemed to be talking knowledgeably as if he knew all about ghosts, witches, and their evening plans. "Santya saw her once – walking all alone at night –towards the haunted Peepal tree. What was she doing there alone at that time of the night, I want to know?"

The Peepal tree that Damya was talking about was on the outskirts of the village. There were no dwellings in that part. Ages ago, a woman had been killed there by a wolf. It was believed that the tree had been haunted by the ghost of the woman ever since. Rampurkars always reported strange goings-on, if they dared to pass that way. Sometimes the howls of a wolf were heard there. There were reports of peals of female laughter being heard there. Some had reported the wailing of a woman. Some villagers had been startled by a rustling in the branches on passing from there. One villager had seen a pale face high up in the branches in the dead of night and the sight had so terrified him that he had gone into a state of shock for fifteen whole minutes. All the Rampurkars avoided, as much as possible, going anywhere near the tree at night. They were too scared.

"Ghosts should be more creative, I think. Why not take the form of an old man or a baby or a cat instead of a woman with green eyes? And why green eyes, I would like to know? Just because they happen to be uncommon?"

"I do not try to understand the mind of a ghost. They exist, and that is enough for me," said Damya.

"Do they really exist though? I wonder," I said. "I am pretty sure that they do not. I wonder why we do not see any in the morning. Also, why can't we see them everywhere? Why can't we see them attending school for instance or taking a poop in the fields?" I was letting my mind run off with the numerous questions to which no one had any answers.

"Eh?" said Damya stupidly.

"Why haven't we ever seen a ghost yet in all our eleven years of life?" I asked him.

"Let us go searching for one," suggested Damya, with the familiar mischievous glint in his eye. "The Peepal tree is the best place to find them. Would you be brave enough to accompany me?"

Now the truth is that I am a little unsure about ghosts, witches (and even God). I'm not too sure whether they exist. I'm not too sure whether to believe in them or not. I fear them nevertheless. However, I was in no mood to educate Damya about my uncertainty. I loved to act bravely in front of him and so behaved as if I did not believe a word of his story.

"Of course, I would. There are no ghosts. Has anybody ever seen one?"

"Well Ganya's aunt would qualify as one," said Damya. "She is a witch!"

"But no one really knows whether Ganya's aunt is a witch. She may just be a plain and simple woman with green eyes".

Damya suddenly became excited.

"Ok. If you are so sure about ghosts not existing, then why don't you prove it? Let us bet on this. You go and circle the haunted Peepal tree thrice on a moonless night, and I will admit that you are braver than me. I may also be willing to admit that ghosts do not exist – that is – if you escape unharmed".

There was a pause. I was not expecting this. I had to admit that I was a little wary of ghosts and witches. I was sure that they did not exist. But what if they did? However, I was filled with a false sense of bravado on that hot lazy afternoon when the thought of scary

ghosts seemed far, far away. And so, I agreed to the

bet.

Chapter Six

Word went around in the village that the Sarpanch had asked us all to gather under the mango tree. The villagers immediately left their work and collected under the mango tree. The Sarpanch cleared his throat noisily and began:

"Now the Government of India, when going through its records, has suddenly realised that our village has not had a Science teacher for a very long time. Since our country has plenty of Science teachers available in various corners of the world, the Government has decided to dispatch an available one to Rampur immediately. Rampur will finally be getting a Science teacher. The new Science teacher is called Mr. Harish, and he will be teaching Science to all the children in the village school. Since none of us know anything about Science, Mr. Harish will be willing to explain the basics of Science to the adults too. Mr. Harish is highly educated. It is rumoured that he has job offers from all the great and good countries of the world and yet he has chosen to live and work in Rampur".

We went on staring at the Sarpanch stupidly. It took some time to process what he had said. One by one, the smiles started to appear on the faces of the Rampurkars. A Science teacher for Rampur! This was exciting. I have always had a lot of curiosity about Science, but no one could really tell me what it was all about. Finally, I will decipher the Science mystery.

Amma seemed to be having similar thoughts.

"See Jambhula", said Amma whispered, "Mr Harish is the one that you now rush to with all your questions". She seemed to be relieved that she would no longer have to struggle with all my questions.

This almost sounded too good to be true. Someone who would be able to answer all my questions! What could be better than that?

Mr. Harish, the Science teacher, arrived in Rampur almost immediately after the announcement was made. One day after, to be precise. There was a lot of curiosity about him in the village. Everyone wanted to see what a Science teacher looked like because no one had seen one before. I tagged along with a few other villagers and went to meet Mr. Harish. Lanky with a goatee and thick spectacles, Mr. Harish seemed to have a similar problem with his hair that I had. He seemed unable to be able to control it, with the result that certain wisps, curls, and frizzes flew this way and that. I liked the look of him.

The Baba somehow was not part of the excitement surrounding Mr. Harish. Neither did he participate in any of the conversation about Mr. Harish nor did he go to meet him after he arrived, as far as I know.

"Are you all ready for some Science?" said Mr. Harish grinning widely from one ear to another. "I know that I have come here to teach the kids, but adults are welcome in my classes too. I have heard that you have had no access to Science for several years. That is the saddest thing that I have ever heard. But don't worry too much. We will soon have Rampur changed in no time at all". The wide grin was back on his face as soon as he finished talking.

We all could sense his excitement and could not help feeling excited ourselves. Science was about to enter our lives!

Our lessons started the next day itself. It was decided to hold the lessons in the evening so that the adults could join in too. The darkies and the fair ones, the adults and the young ones, all would learn Science together. The fair ones huddled together in a group near the mango tree while the darkies sat behind unobtrusively. We were a little hesitant initially. What exactly was this Science? Was it too complicated? We were a bit nervous. Keshavnath summoned some courage and asked Mr. Harish.

"Err, Mr. Harish, if you could start by explaining just what exactly this Science business is, we would be very happy. We just want to know what Science is and then we can go back to our daily lives and not worry about it anymore."

"Oh no, no, no. Once Science gets hold of you, it will not let go so easily," said Mr. Harish rubbing his hands in glee. We felt even more apprehensive. Then he continued a little more seriously. "You can see Science all around you. There is nothing scary about Science. The more you understand it, the more you will use it and love it and the easier your life will be".

We nodded our heads vigorously. He then started to throw at us, one baffling question after another.

"Let me ask you a question. If I throw one of you and an elephant from the same cliff into the water, which one of you will hit the water first?"

"Err – which one of us are you planning to throw, Mr. Harish?" asked Ramdev shaking his head and grinning widely.

"Let us say that I decide to throw you Ramdev, alongside the elephant. Which one of you will hit the water first?" said Mr. Harish. Ramdev beamed, pleased to be chosen for the honour. But he did not know the answer to the question.

We all started mumbling amongst ourselves. I thought that the elephant would hit the water first because it was much heavier. As I found out, most of the other Rampurkars thought the same.

"The elephant" we all chorused loudly.

"Uh-huh", said Mr. Harish, wagging his finger from side to side. "You have got that wrong. Both Ramdev and the elephant will hit the water at the same time", he disclosed. "Now what does this reveal? C'mon, c'mon people, I want answers".

We looked a little blankly at one another. Finally, Mr. Harish revealed the answer himself.

"This experiment proves that lighter objects DO NOT fall faster than heavier ones, as one would think. That is because the gravity of the earth accelerates all objects equally. This fact was discovered by a bloke called Galileo ages ago who proved this by throwing two balls of different weights off the top of a tower. Even though the balls had different weights, they hit the water at the same time".

We all nodded our heads in wonder. I understood that objects of different weights would fall to the ground at the same time when thrown from the same height. However, what was gravity? What was acceleration? These terms bounced right off our heads.

Then a few minutes later Mr. Harish asked – "why does an apple fall DOWN to the ground and not UP?' We listened to him in bewildered silence.

No worries, a fellow called Newton had found the answer to this problem. The apple is pulled to the ground by the gravitational force of the earth. There was the term gravity again. What exactly was gravity? How exactly did the earth exert this force? What exactly was the earth?

A knowing expression came into Mr. Harish eyes. He probably realised that he would have a lot of work to do in educating us in the marvels of Science. His eyes gleamed making him look a little mad. He did not seem to be daunted by the challenge but seemed to look forward to it.

When our village first discovered that the earth (or the world as we thought of it then) was not flat but round like a ball we were astounded. It seemed that this fact had been discovered by a bloke called Pythagoras ages ago. Pythagoras discovered this and a great man called Aristotle managed to prove it. Mr. Harish dutifully and beautifully explained it all to us. He also explained that it was the sun that was the centre of the solar system and the earth went around the sun. Mr. Harish had lighted a *diya* in the centre to portray the sun and marbles all around it to show the various planets. Aiyyo! Would wonders never cease? We were very excited to learn this. We had numerous questions.

Mr. Harish went on revealing one fascinating fact after another.

"Our ancestors were apes! We have evolved from apes. Darwin says so." There was a minute's silence. It took a while for the news to sink in. Then there was a buzz. This could not be true, could it? Apes and humans? No, it could not. This was truly baffling. Mr. Harish showed us books which showed how human beings evolved from apes. The Rampurkars shook their heads in wonder.

The questions continued – from both sides. Mr. Harish patiently answered all our queries. We then asked him a few more. He drew pictures to explain his points. There was a lot of excited chatter. I was so happy! What a stunning discovery! What a great man this Darwin and all the other scientists must have been.

"It was Copernicus who first discovered that earth is a planet and circles the sun. However, this was only a guess, and he had no proof. In Science, everything must have proof. There MUST be evidence." Said Mr. Harish banging his fist on the tree behind him. "Nothing is accepted just because someone said so – however powerful he or she may be." Mr. Harish continued. I particularly liked this aspect of Science. There were no big or small people in Science. There were no bullies. No one was powerful or powerless. No one was dark, and no one was fair. You had to prove what you were saying; only then would it be accepted as a fact.

"Galileo build a powerful instrument called the telescope. This enabled him to see the surface of the moon. Now, how many of you think that the moon is perfect, smooth and round?" Mr. Harish asked. Almost everyone put up their hands.

"You are all wrong. The moon is full of craters. It is not smooth at all. Galileo proved it by looking at it through his telescope."

Another buzz went around the villagers. Is the moon not smooth? Who would have thought? This was all very fascinating. One by one, Mr. Harish smoothly demolished all our pre-conceived notions and replaced them by plain and simple scientific facts.

Mr. Harish also told us about the brilliant scientists that India had produced. One of them was Sushruta, who had performed a nose surgery years ago. He was known as the Father of Surgery in India because of his knowledge of the human body and surgery. He would reconstruct broken noses, arms, and legs.

Mr. Harish also told us about the great Aryabhatta who was an astronomer and a mathematician. The first satellite that India launched was named the Aryabhatta in his honour. There was C.V Raman who was awarded a prestigious award called 'The Nobel Prize' in Physics. There was Homi Bhabha who is known as the father of the nuclear power. (Mr. Harish promised that he would soon give us an introduction to nuclear power as soon as our basic concepts in Science were clear). Then there was Jagadish Chandra Bose, who said that plants could feel pain. (This interested me immensely as I had similar views).

We, Rampurkars puffed up with pride. So many of our own, Indians, had been considered great in the field of Science. All of us immediately started congratulating one another.

Mr. Harish gave numerous experiments for the children to perform.

Experiment One: How to make an egg float in water

What you'll need:

- One egg
- Water
- Salt
- A container

Instructions:

1. First, put an egg in a container half filled with water. See if it floats. It won't.

2. Then stir in lots of salt (about 6 tablespoons) in the water held in the container.

3. Carefully pour in plain water until the container is nearly full (be careful to not disturb or mix the salty water with the plain water).

4. Gently lower the egg into the water and watch what happens.

What happens here?

On adding salt to the water, the salty water becomes dense. It is, therefore, easier for an egg to float in the salty water. When the egg reaches the salty water in the container, it will float.

Experiment Two: How to make an orange sink and float in water

What you'll need

- One orange
- Water
- A container

Instructions:

1. Fill the container with water.

2. Put the orange in the water. The orange will float.

3. Peel the rind from the orange and try the experiment again. The orange will sink.

What happens here?

The rind of an orange is full of holes filled with air. The orange with the rind will, therefore, float in water. When the rind is removed, there will be no air pockets. The density of the orange, therefore, will be greater than the density of water, and the orange will sink.

………………<pull out>………………..

We were utterly amazed and pestered Mr. Harish to give us more such experiments. Mr. Harish, with that mad gleam in his eyes, was happy to oblige.

The fascination with Science grew by the day for all of us. When there were too many questions or when a topic had to be explained in detail, Mr. Harish started holding meetings at night. We forgot about sleep. The children and the adults were way too excited.

I had so many questions for Mr. Harish. He patiently answered them all - the one about leaves sprouting from the dead rat (will not happen). Then the one about fattening plants by feeding them rice (will not happen). The one about observing black ants (to continue with the observations). I was simply raring to go and find proof of various fascinating puzzles. I could not wait to discover and invent!

Soon these meetings became a regular thing every evening. We would all gather outside Mr. Harish's place under the Banyan tree, and we would all talk about Science at very basic levels. Both adults and children started to learn Science together. Somebody would make tea (for the fair ones), and over numerous cups of tea, Science topics were discussed. As the word spread, more and more villagers started to join. Someone decided to open a tea stall just outside Mr. Harish's house. The tea stall made good business.

One day when I was walking to the fields to do a poo, I noticed the Baba and the Sarpanch deep in conversation. They did not notice me, and I heard the name of Mr. Harish being mentioned. I hid behind a tree to eavesdrop and heard the Sarpanch say:

"Should we be worried?"

"Nah!" Baba said, and I could hear him scratching some part of his body, most probably his head (I hope!). "It would take much more than a lowly school teacher to have me worried."

I skipped off because the pressure was getting unbearable but thought about what they had said. It was what I had suspected all along. Mr. Harish was not powerful enough to get the Baba worried. What I cannot understand though is why SCIENCE should have the Sarpanch worried?

Very, very slowly the village started to change under Mr. Harish. My dead rat may not have sprouted leaves but the seeds of Science, which were lying dormant for so long, slowly started sprouting in Rampur under Mr. Harish's able guidance. I was not alone in my love of Science. Most of the adults and children in Rampur were getting dazzled by all the new information that Mr. Harish was feeding us with.

Mr. Harish soon started speaking about the importance of being treated by a medically qualified doctor. Our Doctor Sahab was at once relieved and admitted to being a little scared. (Amma explained to me that all of us were not yet used to the pace of change and too many things were happening at once. That can be a little scary).

"Science has researched, investigated, conducted experiments and found proof of the medical procedures. Questions have answers in Science, and these are based on facts. People are still trying to find answers to some questions, but we do know the answers to a lot many of them. It is important to use medicines for certain ailments" said Mr. Harish.

As usual, he elaborated this by telling us all a story. Bacteria are tiny organisms that can cause infection in humans. If you have a severe fever or a severe tummy upset, then it is possible that it is because of a bacterial infection. Years ago, there was a very curious fellow called Fleming. Now Fleming cultivated bacteria in a dish because he wished to study and observe them. Often his studies and experiments went on for several months. One day he decided that he had had enough of the bacteria and decided to go on a holiday. After having a good rest, he was ready to go back to the bacteria. When he rushed to them, he found that a green mold had collected all over the bacteria in the dish. This mold was killing some of the bacteria that he had been growing. He was fascinated. He had inadvertently discovered a way to kill bacteria. Harmful bacteria in humans could, therefore, be destroyed! He grew some more green-mold and discovered that it could kill lots of different bacteria. This green mold was later called penicillin. This was a very important discovery. If you got a deep cut on your body, there are chances that it will get infected with bacteria. If you do not treat it with penicillin, then the infection could spread throughout the body possibly killing you. It is important to treat it on time and to treat it correctly. It is extremely important that a person who has been educated in the Science of medicine treats patients. It is too risky otherwise.

We processed this information. It made a lot of sense. Our tummies sometimes got upset chronically because of the bacteria! Penicillin would be able to destroy the bacteria as found by Fleming. Fascinating! Maybe we should start taking medicines from Doctor Sahab instead of the Baba? After all, how can turning somersaults at four o' clock every day, one of Baba's favourite remedy, help cure a tummy bug? Maybe, just maybe, Baba was not as clever as we all thought him to be?

Mr. Harish went on, day after day, revealing fascinating facts about Science. When he came across a dead frog one day, he brought it to the meetings and then dissected it so that all the villagers could see its internal organs. The butchers and the meat-eaters amongst us had seen the internal organs of animals plenty of times before, but the children were mesmerised to see the heart of the frog. I was too excited even to talk! What strange and utterly fascinating facts Mr. Harish revealed day by day. Every lesson was so stupendous, so awesome that it was unbelievable!

On learning such unique and fascinating facts (for example of the earth being round and not flat), the reaction of the Rampurkars was usually one of the following:

Some of them refused to take this at face value. They decided that there very well may be some truth to the notion but they were simply not willing to accept this as a fact. They would make their own enquiries and experiments and only when fully convinced would they agree with Pythagoras or Galileo or Mr. Harish.

Some of the people were immediately convinced. Mr. Harish did such a thorough job of explaining everything, along with detailed diagrams, that there was absolutely no doubt in their minds. The earth just HAD to be round.

Some of the people simply did not care. Round or flat – what did it matter? They did not care.

There was a fourth group of people (let us call them group 4) which, somehow, had an extremely strange reaction on hearing that the earth was round. They were angry. They were in no mood to hear things that were contrary to what they believed. The earth was flat – that is what they believed, and that is what they would continue to believe. How dare that Pythagoras fellow via Mr. Harish tells them otherwise? This Harish fellow was slicing up dead animals in the name of Science. This should not be allowed. They did not want all these new-fangled ideas. This was simply not done! They were a little scared.

A few days after Mr. Harish's arrival, the village threw a party - to celebrate the fact that the earth was round and all the other fascinating stuff that we had learnt. It did not matter that we had discovered these facts a lot later than all the other people in the world. The important thing was that we had now discovered them. The celebrations went on late at night. People from group 4 did not attend.

Chapter Seven

There was a discussion being held in the village about the evil eye.

What exactly is the evil eye? Is it an eye that goes around walking on its own? Does anyone know what the evil eye is? No. It is just an eye that could cause harm to you.

Has anyone seen the evil eye? No.

Can anyone prove the existence of the evil eye? No.

Is it possible for an eye to exist without a body? No.

Can it be proved that misfortune will come our way because of the evil eye? No.

Why then should we fear it? We would rather believe what can be proved – like in Science. We are no longer going to believe in the evil eye. A few of the villagers confidently made this proclamation while a few other timid ones merely mumbled something inaudible. As was the norm, group 4 was absent from these discussions.

Mr. Harish then made another shocking announcement. Ever since we have been introduced to

Science, it has been one shocking discovery after another. Mr. Harish told us that the miracle of walking over embers that Baba had performed had not been a miracle after all. It had been all Science, and Mr. Harish was going to demonstrate how it was done.

Mr. Harish calmly asked Chiltya to get some coal and light it. Then, again, very calmly, Mr. Harish walked all over the embers – just like Baba had done! He even did a little jig while he was walking on the burning coal. This was no miracle at all. Anyone could do it! Mr. Harish warned the children not to try this on their own, and he then explained the Science behind the 'miracle'. Coal is a bad conductor of heat. If you, therefore, walk quickly across the embers, before they have a chance to really heat up, they will not cause any burns or blisters. It was as simple as that.

I knew it. I had always suspected that there was something more to it.

Rampurkars started to shake their heads in wonder. Ramdeo wondered if he could try walking on the embers.

"Why not?" said Mr. Harish. He carefully checked the condition of the burning coals. Once he was satisfied, he asked Ramdeo to walk on them quickly.

Ramdeo had his eyes shut tight. He clenched his fist, and before anyone could realise what was happening, he had walked over the coals. He then turned to face the others with a big smile on his face.

Rampurkars went on shaking their heads in even more wonder. So, it was true. This was no miracle at all. Baba had fooled them.

Someone went and told Baba about how his miracle had been busted by Mr. Harish. Baba had become livid and had thrown a banana at the person who had brought the news to him.

"I considered Mr. Harish to be an inconsequential Science teacher so far, but this is no longer true. Mr. Harish seems to have most of the villagers in his grip, and he is meddling too much in things that do not concern him. What is this nonsense that the villagers are engaged in? How dare they forget my instructions about farting, burping, somersaults and hen chases to remain happy? How dare they go to the Doctor instead of coming to me?"

Baba had spat out his rage all in one go. Baba had then gone to have a chat with the Sarpanch. According to Damya (who had taken the trouble to follow Baba all the way to the Sarpanch's house), the

Sarpanch was not very happy either. He did not like to see his importance being taken away by someone else. The two had sat together for a long time deciding on the next course of action.

I wonder what plans are brewing between those two, but I am not really that concerned. Mr. Harish was here to sort out all our problems with the help of Science. If we had Science on our side, there was no reason to be afraid.

Meanwhile, Damya kept pestering me about the bet. I wished that I had not agreed to do anything so foolish. I had no intention of going anywhere near the haunted Peeple tree on a moonless night. However, I was also unwilling to accept defeat. I decided to go and have a chat with Mr. Harish.

Mr. Harish already had a group of people with him when I went to visit. That was usually the case.

He was always surrounded by some group or the other having deep discussions about Science.

"Mr. Harish, do ghosts and witches exist?" I blurted out.

"An excellent question," said Mr. Harish, rubbing his hands together, looking around the assembled villagers.

"I have never seen a ghost myself. I, therefore, do not think that they exist, simply because no one has been able to prove that they do. After death, our bodies decompose and turn to dust. That is the end of it, in my opinion".

"But don't you feel scared?" I asked him.

"Scared of what? How can I fear something that does not exist?" said Mr. Harish.

I thought for a moment. Mr. Harish did have a point. What was the use of getting worked up about something which (to the best of my knowledge) did not exist? Then the story of my bet with Damya came tumbling out. I told him that I was a little scared to visit the haunted tree and yet did not want to back out of the dare.

"I will come with you," said Mr. Harish.

"We will come too," said some of the villagers. Now that they had started believing in the miracles of Science, most of them tended to trust Mr. Harish's (and their own) logic and reasoning. "Let us see once and for all whether ghosts exist".

I thought that it was truly a brilliant idea. What could be better than to go with Mr. Harish and a group of people? I would not feel so scared then and would still be able to win the bet.

"I will come and ask your parents for permission. Maybe they would like to join too?" Mr. Harish asked.

Bapu was reluctant to believe in the non-existence of ghosts. However, Amma, brave and sensible at the best of times, was sure that there were no such things as ghosts or witches. She decided to accompany us. Bapu decided to stay at home. We would soon know which one of them had taken the right decision. The plan was made for the next moonless night.

When the night arrived, I could not keep still. Amma had given up on me that day, but she was excited too. A total of fifteen villagers (fair ones and darkies) had decided to accompany us to the haunted tree. At the appointed time, all of us gathered outside Mr. Harish's house. Damya had not been very pleased with the way our plans had turned out. When I had first told him that the rest of the villagers would be accompanying us, he had been a little glum.

"The bet had been for you to go there alone to prove how brave you were" he said petulantly.

I insisted that the bet had been for me to circle the haunted tree at night thrice and that was all that mattered. Damya still thought that it was a little unfair, but he could not stay glum for long. Slowly the excitement caught him too. Would we see a ghost at night?

The entire troupe set off towards the Peepal tree. We were in good spirits (if you can excuse the pun) when we started off. It was a walk of almost fifteen minutes to the haunted tree. The atmosphere decidedly turned a little eerie as soon as we left the safety of the village and entered the outskirts. There was no one around. No huts, no people, just some desolate trees scattered here and there. The silence and the darkness were a little unnerving. I was glad to have Amma and others with me. I had to admit that I would have never been able to do this on my own.

"Are you scared?" I asked Amma, curious to know her answer.

"Not at all. I have been confident all along that ghosts do not exist. This will just prove my point," she said determinedly.

Mr. Harish was about to say something when suddenly we heard the piercing howl of a wolf. The howl was so loud in the silent night that all of us must have jumped, as a group, at least two feet off the ground. Damya was so scared that he scampered off like a frightened hen. We were a little unsure as to what to do, but Mr. Harish calmly continued to walk. I was alarmed. However, there was no backing out now. I was also feeling rather pleased about the fact that Damya had scampered off. I would now be able to tease him mercilessly about this.

"Just a wolf howling somewhere. Nothing to get excited about," said Mr. Harish reassuringly. We followed him somewhat reluctantly.

We were now very close to the tree. Was that a rustling that I could hear? It was becoming very difficult to be brave. All of us (except perhaps Mr. Harish and Amma) were extremely alert to the slightest of sounds. All of us (except perhaps Mr. Harish and Amma) were ready to bolt at the slightest hint of any disturbance. All of us (including Mr. Harish and Amma) kept looking up at the Peeple tree. Damya had sheepishly re-joined us. I gave him a triumphant look but was too tense to do anything else.

"I don't know what came over me", he whispered to me, and despite all my fear I laughed at him.

Mr. Harish went and sat right under the haunted tree. He had got a blanket which he now spread under the tree and waved to us to join him. Tentatively, one by one, we went and sat on the blanket. We kept looking up at the tree from time to time. I kept looking behind me as well. I did not want the arms of a witch to throttle me from behind. Damya refused to join us! He still believed passionately in ghosts. He stood a little way off, ready to bolt at once if required.

We felt a little better (only just) once we all were seated.

"See, this is just like any other tree", said Mr. Harish. "There are no ghosts here".

Little by little, we started to relax. Keshavnath came up with the idea of holding a jokes competition. The person who came up with the best joke would be crowned the winner. Even from a distance, I could see Damya perk up when he heard the word 'jokes'. His knowledge about fart jokes was legendary. He would not want to miss the opportunity to share his jokes with the others.

We soon got into the mood of things. Each joke was followed by loud laughter. Rambhau guffawed so loudly that his laugh alone would have scared off any lurking ghost. So much so that even Damya forgot to get scared. He came and joined us under the tree and started off with one joke after another, sometimes accompanied by live demonstrations. We had a very enjoyable time and forgot all about the ghosts and witches. Kashinath was declared the winner for telling the best joke. His joke had been so funny that Damya had held his tummy and chuckled away so much that it ended up giving him a tummy ache.

"Shall we leave now?" asked Mr. Harish after some time.

A ghost or a witch (had one existed) would have made an appearance by now. It was decided it was time to go home. I quickly got up and circled the tree thrice. Everyone clapped. I had won the bet! Damya admitted that I had won. It had been that easy.

We headed home – a little tired but jubilant. A worried Bapu was waiting for us.

"Did you see any?" he asked in a whisper.

"Bah! Ghosts – they do not exist," said Amma firmly.

"Yes, Bapu – you should have accompanied us. Ghosts and witches simply do not exist," I told him confidently.

Chapter Eight

To be gripped by a fear of ghosts and then to realise

that the fear was baseless was deeply empowering. I

no longer fear ghosts and witches. They do not exist. I

felt like shouting from the house-tops. I DO NOT

FEAR GHOSTS AND WITCHES BECAUSE THEY DO NOT EXIST.

I have been making such fascinating discoveries ever since Mr. Harish arrived in this sleepy village of ours. Yesterday the most amazing thing happened to me. I was tinkering about with a piece of mirror. Suddenly the sun's rays caught the mirror, and my hand nearly got burnt, so strong were the rays. A dry leaf that was lying next to the mirror caught fire. I stared at it in silence, but a million ideas were whirring around in my head. How could this have happened? I had managed to create fire with just a piece of old mirror! It was unbelievable. I was so fascinated that I carried out the same process again and then yet again. It worked every time. I burnt several dry leaves in the process. I felt a strange kind of power – I had discovered the ability to create fire with just a simple mirror, and it felt great.

I rushed to discuss this with Mr. Harish. He explained how the mirror focussed all the sun's rays onto a single point thereby causing a flame. He told me about the powerful energy of the sun called the solar energy and how it could be harnessed for different things. It was all extremely fascinating. It also got me thinking. I wanted to harness the solar energy too. Was that possible? I was thinking of ways in which I could use it. Could the sun be used to cook food for instance without using coal or any other fuel?

"Why not?" said Mr. Harish when I asked him about it. Try and develop a contraption that will use the energy of the sun to cook rice", Mr. Harish said.

The task that he had set for me overwhelmed me initially. However, the more I thought of it, the easier it got. I had already used the sun's energy to make fire. Now all I had to was to use that fire somehow to cook rice. That would not be too difficult. Would it? This experiment consumed me. I thought about it day after day. So much so, that I forgot to eat sometimes. My entire day was taken up in thinking of contraptions to harness the energy of the sun to cook rice. I got hold of some tools from Bapu. I had to somehow combine a mirror with a container which could be used to hold some rice. I came up with many ways of doing this. It wasn't easy, but I persevered. It was things like these that made me happy.

It was during this time that Mr. Harish, with some help from the Government of India, decided to hold a blood donation camp in the village. He made an announcement in the village asking for volunteers to donate blood. We all were a little scared. Donate blood? Why? What was the need? All of us immediately rushed to Mr. Harish with questions, who, as had become the norm, was happy to clarify.

"If a person becomes deficient in blood due to some reason then blood from another person can be pumped into the body to cover up the deficiency. However, for this to work, the blood must be of the same type. For example, if a person has blood type 'A' and you put blood type 'B' in his body then this is not going to work. People with blood type 'A' can only donate blood to people with blood type 'A'. The only exception is blood type 'O', which can be donated to a person of any blood type. All volunteers would have their blood type noted and recorded. Their donated blood would be stored with the blood of the same type. Two distinct types of blood would not be mixed together."

All of us kept looking at him with our eyes open. Blood pumped out from one person into another! Marvellous! Is there no end to the wonders of Science?

On the appointed day, the vans of the people from the Government started arriving in the morning. Tables and equipment were laid out. Doctors and nurses sent by the Government of India were ready with their injections. Bottles were ready. Each type of blood would be tested and results stored. If anyone required a particular blood type, then the blood of the person with the relevant blood type could be used. It was as simple as that. The children were exempt from this. I was disappointed. I wanted to see what my blood looked like in a bottle.

"But why are children exempt?" I asked Mr. Harish.

Mr. Harish explained that since children were still growing, they did not have sufficient blood to donate.

One by one the villagers queued up. I was surprised to see the Holy Baba leading the queue. Some of the villagers were gossiping that the Baba was donating blood simply to get into the good books of the Government of India. I was watching his reaction intently. When the needle went in his podgy arm, he gave a loud yelp and closed his eyes shut like a baby.

"Is it over? Is it over?" he repeatedly asked like a child. He saw his own blood in the bottle and nearly fainted.

Most of the villagers got their blood identified. The Holy Baba was astounded to learn that he shared a blood type with Bapu. He was under the impression that his blood type would only be shared by people as important as him. To have an inconsequential darkie share a blood type with him was too much for him to bear.

Mr. Harish jumped at the opportunity and took his chance to share his knowledge further. He explained that even though we may look different from the outside, we are essentially the same from the inside. If Baba needed to be given blood for some medical reason, then it would be my Bapu (or anyone having the same blood type as the Baba or anyone having blood type 'O') who would be able to give him blood.

I took the opportunity to say loudly to Baba and to everyone who could hear- "A darkie's blood is the same as that of anyone else". The Baba gave me a lethal look whereas Mr. Harish only smiled.

Chapter Nine

Rampurkar was changing rapidly. After our nocturnal
adventures searching for ghosts, even firm ghost
believers like Bapu stopped believing in ghosts.
Prompted by the stories of the people who had been
there, the rest of the villagers decided to go and see for

108

themselves. They went, and nothing happened. No ghost turned up. With the result that the villagers no longer avoided the outskirts as they once did. Now that the area was accessible, a few of them even decided to build huts and started cultivating their crops there. The ever enterprising Lalnath decided to open a tea stall there. It became an adda for villagers to collect and gossip. Lalnath's tea stall, even though it was on the outskirts, became very popular. Everyone forgot about ghosts and witches.

Soon the Rampurkars started to question Baba's solutions to their problems. How can performing somersaults in quick succession prevent cows from running away? What was the connection between the two events? How can plucking out three grey hairs cure a donkey? How can giving loud burps ensure the birth of more piglets? Where was the logic? There was no Science in this. The solutions provided by the Baba were simply barmy. He probably was making up all this as he went along. Rampurkars now knew enough about Science to understand that the Baba was just spouting nonsense.

In short, we had all started to think scientifically and logically. We refused to take anything at face value. We needed proof and evidence to believe. Most of the Rampurkars now started to visit Doctor Sahab for their ailments. Doctor Sahab was no longer the anxious, nervous doctor that he had been in the past. With the village becoming more scientific and logical, he was no longer worried. He happily treated all the patients. Mr. Harish was always there to further boost his confidence.

Mr. Harish lectures on Science continued. He continued to provide us with fascinating scientific facts daily. We started to get addicted to our daily Science fix. Some Rampurkars were so fascinated that, like me, they started conducting their own experiments. They wanted to invent, create and explore. They wanted to discover. People started to forget to pay respects to the Baba. They forgot to fear the Sarpanch. They were so busy! There was an entire world of Science waiting to be discovered by them, and we were raring to go.

Baba continued to hold his weekly sessions. The villagers, who attended, mostly attended out of habit. Group 4 though, were staunch supporters of the Baba and continued to believe in him. The Baba was disturbed to see the numbers dwindling day by day. During one of the sessions, the solution given by him was questioned by one of the villagers.

"But how will standing on my head ensure that I will be happy?"

For once, Baba did not have an answer. He was not used to being questioned. The villagers noted this.

The numbers at Baba's problem solving sessions continued to dwindle until one day nobody except the Group 4 attended. No one else was present at Baba's session anymore. The villagers did not believe in his solutions, and they were too busy with their experiments and discovery of Science.

And then calamity struck! Rampur witnessed a devastating earthquake. It happened in the middle of the night when we were sleeping. The ground trembled and shook. The dogs started to howl. The semi-solid roofs started shaking, and bits and pieces started to fall off. Luckily people woke up due to all the noise and ran outside their huts. However, a few still got injured by the falling tin sheets that they had stacked on the roof. Some of them were injured because of falling branches. Some of the animals from the village ran off never to be found causing great grievance to their owners. No one died and none were seriously injured, but there was a lot of damage. Everyone went around looking extremely forlorn.

There was a steady stream of villagers to Doctor Sahab that day. A few were in shock to find the earth shaking under them. Some of them had injured an arm; others had injured a leg. Some of them had injured their heads. Luckily the injuries were not major. Damya and I had managed to escape unhurt.

Baba then came up with something that was very worrying indeed. "The earthquake happened because you have been neglecting my instructions," he proclaimed. Soon the word spread. The earthquake happened because the Baba was displeased.

Mr. Harish patiently explained that earthquakes were caused when the rocks that were underground suddenly broke. The sudden release of energy caused the ground to tremble and shake. The villagers understood his explanation. However, doubt had been planted in their minds. Was it possible that the earthquake was caused due to the wrath of Baba? Should they leave Science alone for a while?

Mr. Harish explained to the villagers that the Baba or any human do not have the power to cause earthquakes. Earthquakes were a natural phenomenon, and the Baba was just taking them all for a ride by suggesting otherwise. However, the villagers were still reeling from the after-effects of the earthquake and did not know quite what to believe.

Knowing that the villagers were a little doubtful about the causes of the earthquake, the Baba and Sarpanch decided to make the most of this opportunity and decided to hold a meeting.

The Baba ranted for nearly three hours! A further calamity is about to fall Rampur, he said. You have seen the havoc that the earthquake caused. That was just a warning. He told them that he had had a dream in which it was revealed that further calamity and death and destruction would come their way if the villagers did not mend their ways and go back to the old style of living.

Mr. Harish was shaking his head in sadness.

Then the Sarpanch took over. What he announced next stunned us out of our minds. He informed the villagers that evil Science had taken a strong hold of their lives and this was what was causing all the damage. To prevent further damage, he had decided to ban Science from the village of Rampur.

"By the powers bestowed upon me, I now declare this village Science free. No more Science, no more experiments, no more questions. I have been told by the Baba that if this nonsense is not stopped at once, then a great calamity will befall Rampur, one from which the village will never recover. From this moment on, Science has now been banned from Rampur".

Science has been banned from Rampur.

Science has been banned from Rampur.

Science has been banned from Rampur.

These unbelievable words echoed in my mind long after the Sarpanch had said them. The Baba watched our distress rubbing his oily hands together.

116

Mr. Harish looked thunderstruck like most of the villagers.

But there was more. Anyone found engaging in Science, doing whacky experiments or even talking about Science would have their little toe chopped off.

There was a stunned silence. Little toe chopped off? Some villagers started getting angry. What was this nonsense? These people were elected by them. India was a democratic country. There should be no threats about chopping off people's toes in this country.

There was still more. Science will be banned from all schools. Since a Science teacher would no longer be required, Mr. Harish was free to pack up his bags and move to some other corner of India.

All of us (except perhaps Group 4) were really distressed. We liked Mr. Harish and looked upon him as a friend. We could not afford to lose him and all his valuable lessons. I was devastated. It was only Mr. Harish who could help me with all my experiments.

After the initial silence, everyone started to speak at once. Everyone wanted to offer their opinion. Group 4 took the opportunity to make their distaste for Science known. Others fought for Science.

"Science is harmless"

"Science has the power to destroy"

"Science is fascinating"

"Science is evil"

"Why not stick to what we know?"

"Science is so cool"

"Old ways are boring. We need to change"

"I cannot wait to invent and explore"

Until the Baba held up his hand and thundered. "My dear people. You do not have an option. No, you certainly do not have an option", and so saying he left rubbing his oily palms and shaking his podgy head. I noticed a few warts growing on it.

The Sarpanch and the entire Gram Panchayat came on. "We have deliberated on this topic a lot. We cannot allow the village to suffer" – was the unanimous decision of the Gram Panchayat.

"But we are not suffering" interjected someone.

"Silence! I cannot allow this village to destroy itself".

Then the group 4 bullies thundered. "Woe betides anyone found to engage in evil Science. Their little toes will be chopped off", they repeated in glee.

"What nonsense was this? How can anyone threaten us like this?"

The Panchayat members simply did not believe in or understand Science. They only wanted the people to follow the Baba so that they could control them.

"I'm afraid that this is the way things are going to be from now on. Indulge in Science and have your toe chopped off". Nothing anyone said made them change their minds. Science had been banned from the village of Rampur.

Initially, some people decided to be brave. They cannot chop off toes like this. Let us see what they can do, they said. However, their bravado was short-lived. People from group 4 menacingly went around the village with big sickles in their hands keeping a watch on everyone. These sickles would be used to chop little toes. No one was allowed to read Science books. No one could study Science. No one could even discuss Science. How would we be able to live without Science?

Chapter Ten

What gives the Sarpanch the right to take away

Science from everyone's lives? I was fuming and

miserable at the same time. I had to have Science in

my life. Bapu told me that Sarpanchs are meant to be

the voice of the people. They get elected by the people.

But how can this Sarpanch be the voice of the people when most Rampurkars want and need Science? What right does he have? And just who do these people moving around with sickles think they are? Rampur had always been such a peaceful village. We never had people moving around threateningly ever before this. Rampur is changing for the worst!

We had been having so much fun with Science until it was brutally snatched away from us. Even though there was still a lot of fight left in me, I felt listless and bored and did not feel like getting out of my blanket in the morning. Though school continued as usual, it was just not the same without my favourite subject and favourite teacher. It was simply one boring day after another. I was eager to complete my experiment on solar energy but was too scared of losing my toe.

I decided to go and meet Mr. Harish. I went over to Damya's house to ask whether he wanted to come too.

Damya was busy picking his nose. He was digging deep and then gazing lovingly at the piece of treasure that he had dug up.

"Damya, let us go and talk to Mr Harish," I said.

"What on earth for? Do you want your toe chopped off?"

"No harm in just chatting, is there?"

Damya was not interested. He did not miss Science as I did. He was happy and content with himself, unlike me.

I went to Mr. Harish's house alone. The goons from Group 4 were patrolling about. They glared at me when they saw me go in. Surely, they were not going to eavesdrop on every conversation to prevent people from discussing Science? Thankfully, they did not.

"I am glad to see you Jambhula," said Mr. Harish.

I looked at him and did not know how to say everything that I had to say. I do not need to. Mr. Harish had something to say to me.

"There is going to be the annual village Science competition for children to be held in Seetapur. Children from all the nearby villages will be attending. Rampur has never ever participated because as you know Science had never been a part of this village. However, this time I would like you to represent Rampur".

He said it just like that without even lowering his voice.

"Mr. Harish, Mr. Harish. Please keep your voice down. There are people moving around with sickles, all ready to chop little toes, outside", I said spluttering and gasping. I looked out of the window. Talking about Science was forbidden. What was Mr. Harish thinking?

Mr. Harish continued calmly. "Every participant has to carry out an experiment of their choice and explain the reasoning behind it. I am pretty sure that you will do well with the experiment on solar energy that you are working on".

"Mr. Harish, please lower your voice. I do not want us to lose our toes", I said in a whisper.

However, as I started to take in what he was saying, I lost my fear a little. A Science competition! How grand it would be to participate on behalf of Rampur. I really wanted to. But then, almost immediately, I started to feel gloomy and fearful again.

"But what about the goons? The Sarpanch and the Baba? The Gram Panchayat?" I asked Mr. Harish.

"They do not need to know. If your parents agree, then I will enter your name in the competition. You start thinking about the experiment that you want to perform. I will give you my full cooperation."

I really wasn't expecting a grown up to behave like this. Mr. Harish wanted me to take part in the Science competition secretly without letting anyone else (other than my parents) know! He really must love Science to go against the Sarpanch like this.

Furthermore, out of all the children, he had chosen me!

That thrilled me to the core.

"I am not afraid Jambhula because I am not

doing anything wrong. I have been thinking of ways to

get Science back in this village ever since it was

banned", said Mr. Harish.

Amma and Bapu were reluctant to let me take

part. They did not want me to lose my little toe. They

feared losing theirs as well. They also thought that Mr.

Harish would lose one (if not both) toes too if he kept

on with these Science related activities.

Mr. Harish decided to come and talk to my

parents. He convinced them that whatever happened he

would ensure that I would not lose my toe. He would

look after his own toes as well. All our toes would be

safe. He guaranteed.

I had hidden the tools and other paraphernalia required for my experiment beneath a hole behind the hut. After our conversation, I continued to work secretly on my experiment. I had designed a box, the top of which was entirely covered with a mirror. The mirror would concentrate all the sun's energy. The box could be opened, and pots and pans could be kept inside it. The lid of the box would be shut, and the food would be cooked with solar energy. That was my plan. I still wasn't there yet, and there was a lot that remained to be done.

I thought about the competition every day. I was by now so desperate to take part that I was almost ready to lose a toe if required. I wanted to show the children from nearby villages my experiment about harnessing solar energy. If this was going to be at the cost of losing my toe, then so be it.

After realising how crazy both of us were about Science, my parents finally agreed to let me participate. It was decided. I would take part in the Science competition.

Chapter Eleven

Different villagers reacted to the Science ban

differently. Some of them, like the people from group

4, had always mistrusted Science and were glad to get

rid of it. A few of them were confused. If calamities

were caused due to people following Science, then it

was best to not indulge too much in it. However, their logical minds kept telling them otherwise. Calamities like the earthquake could not be caused due to humans misbehaving. Mr. Harish had almost drilled that into them.

Most of the Science-loving folks went into a kind of mourning. Their passion had been cruelly snatched away from them. They missed Science. A lot. Some of them even dreamt about it at night. Their life had seemed to have had a purpose when they had discovered Science. Their ambitions had soared at the limitless possibilities the subject had offered. Several Rampurkars had made up their minds to go out to other cities that offered more facilities to explore this fascinating topic further. Some of them were planning new inventions, and now all this had been taken away from them.

The power of the Baba went on increasing yet again. Group 4 started to prevent the villagers from going to Doctor Sahab. They would stand outside Doctor Sahab's door, sickles in hand. People, therefore, started flocking to Baba again albeit reluctantly. Baba told them that everything would now be all right. The calamity would no longer befall them. People started doing headstands, somersaults, burping and farting and everything else the Baba asked them to do. However, their minds were simply not in it. Mr. Harish had previously managed to convince them that these things were mere superstitions and no calamity would befall them if they did not do these things. Rampurkars could therefore no longer believe in these superstitions even if they wanted to. However, they were also scared of losing their little toe, and so they carried on listlessly. The rule of fear had taken over Rampur, and no one really knew what to do about it.

Mr. Harish was now jobless. He knew that he should be making arrangements to leave Rampur to take up a job elsewhere. However, his heart was simply not in it. Just like he had benefitted the Rampurkars by opening their eyes to the wonders of Science, he himself had benefitted too by the diligence and fascination of his students – both adults and children – in the subject. He had so become a part of Rampur that he had started to believe that this was his home. He could not think of leaving this and going to some other town.

He tried talking to the Sarpanch. However, the Sarpanch was adamant. He was convinced that no good would come of meddling in Science. Everything had changed! No, no, he could not risk that. Science remained banned in the village. The Sarpanch and Mr. Harish had taken such a dislike to each other that they knew that it was pointless to argue any further.

Now it so happened, that one day, a large storm occurred in Rampur. It poured and raged and thundered for the full week. The tiny village got flooded. Some farms were destroyed. A few huts were destroyed. The storm caused havoc especially because it went on and on. Livestock ran away never to be found. Some of them drowned. The Rampurkars were miserable. They would have to start all over again.

A village meeting was held that evening. Mr. Harish was present along with the Baba and Sarpanch.

"I would like to ask one question to the Baba," said Mr. Harish loudly. The villagers gasped. No one had dared talk to Baba in such a loud voice. "If the earthquake took place because of indulging in Science then why has the storm taken place now that Science has been banned? We have totally given up Science. What is the reason for this storm then?"

The assembled group grew silent. Not one murmur from anyone. No one knew what to say. Mr. Harish's logical question had got everyone thinking.

"How dare you speak to me like that?" said the Baba. He huffed and puffed for a while and then was silent. Mr. Harish calmly sat down. He had made his point.

The Sarpanch was not willing to give up this easily. "There may be a few villagers who are still engaging in Science secretly. This storm could have been caused by them. If so, my people will soon find them", he thundered.

When I heard the Sarpanch say that I could not stop shaking. Was he aware of my scientific activity? Did he suspect anything? I caught Mr. Harish's eye, and he gave me a reassuring look. Fervently, I hoped that my hiding place where I had hidden all my Science goods, would not be discovered.

Slowly, bit by bit the Rampurkars got back on track. The storm subsided. Houses were repaired. Farms were made functional again. Wounds were healed. However, these were not the Rampurkars of old, now that Science had touched them. Several of them had started to see through the Sarpanch and the Baba. They realised that both were simply big bullies who were fond of sweet laddus at the villager's expense. They should not be allowed to get away with it.

There was a lot going on behind closed doors. We could not gather together as a group without arousing suspicion. So, we passed on the word from one to another. And word spread fast. We had decided to protest the Science ban. We would all peacefully rebel if the ban was not revoked. If the Sarpanch did not listen to us, then we would use the tactic adopted by the great Mahatma and engage in peaceful non-cooperation. No one would till the farms. The single solitary shop of the village would remain closed. No milk would be supplied. No fruit and vegetables would be sold. No tea would be sold in the tiny village tea shop. This was the path that would be taken if the Sarpanch refused to listen. We would suffer, but we were willing to do that for Science.

There was still a year left until the Gram Panchayat elections could be held. The villagers encouraged Mr. Harish to stand for the Sarpanch elections. No one trusted the current Sarpanch and his bullying ways anymore. Mr. Harish was assured of our full support. Mr. Harish was by now so in love with Rampur that he agreed.

On Mr. Harish's suggestion, it was decided to hold the peaceful protest for Science on the day of the Science competition. Of course, the villagers were totally unaware of the existence of the Science competition, but Mr. Harish ensured that the villagers would hold the protest on the day of the competition. Mr. Harish had agreed to accompany me to the competition, and as the goons would be busy in tackling the protest, it would give us sufficient time to slip away without arousing suspicion. That was his plan.

Ramdev, whose uncle was an employee of the Government of India, decided to request his uncle to come over to Rampur on the day of the protest. The Sarpanch's high-handedness must be brought to the notice of the Government of India. The villagers hoped that the Government of India would take some stern action against the Sarpanch's bullying and let him know in no uncertain terms that he could not ban

Science from the villagers' life just because he felt like

it.

Chapter Twelve

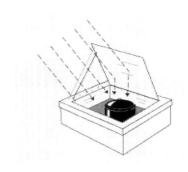

Mr. Harish had explained that the world's first solar oven was invented by a man from Switzerland called Horace de Saussure in 1767 and here I am trying to do the same. The box had been designed and assembled. The top of the box had been painted black. Since black surfaces tend to get very hot, it would enable the box to convert sunlight into heat energy. The pot that I was going to place inside the solar cooker had also been painted black. I had designed another insulated box inside the first one. The pot would be placed inside this smaller box. This smaller box would let in sunlight and would trap the heat inside the box. The inner lid of the outer box had been covered by a mirror, which when kept open, would reflect extra sunshine inside the box. Any food placed inside the pot would get cooked by the energy of the sun in a few hours. So, there it was. My newly designed solar cooker! Ta-Da!

I had worked on my experiment every day for all of two months. It had been a fascinating project. Mr. Harish ensured that I had fully understood the Science behind it. I am so proud of my solar cooker. I do not really care whether I win or not. I had a wonderful time doing it. The project was such a secret that I could not even take Damya into confidence. There were times when I felt like blurting out the secret, but I did not. It was too risky.

On the day of the protest, Rampurkars had already started to gather in the morning. They were holding placards in their hands:

"We need Science"

"Science is the future"

"Science is progress"

"Science should not be banned"

"We love Science"

"Our demand is to have Science returned to us"

"Revoke the Science ban"

What fun they were all going to have. Come to think of it; it would be tough to chop off EVERYONE'S little toes. There were too many people involved in the protest. And how would they chop off the toe when Doctor Sahab was on our side? They cannot possible go around chopping people's toes with the silly sickles that they had been carrying around the village. India is a democratic country. The Government of India and the People of India would not let it happen.

Soon the protests started. Everyone had gathered right outside the Sarpanch's office, shouting loud slogans. Sarpanch, Baba and group 4 were taken completely by surprise and were too stunned to react. Rampurkars had been so compliant in the past that no one had expected them to actively rebel. That too for Science! Ramdev's uncle had arrived with a few more of his friends from the Government of India. They were silently watching the protests. One of his friends worked for a national newspaper. He was busy making notes about the protests.

I had started to feel a little nervous. Mr. Harish was to meet me outside the bus station. I did not have to wait long and could see his frizzy hair in the distance. Thankfully there were no goons from Group 4 lurking around. All of them were busy in managing the protest. Mr. Harish's plan had worked. No one noticed us slipping away.

We took the bus to Seetapur and arrived after a few minutes. A huge tent had been erected there.

"THE ANNUAL SCIENCE COMPETITION FOR CHILDREN" screamed a hoarding. There were lots of children holding their projects and accompanied by their parents or teachers. I saw some big eyes, some nervous faces and other smiling faces looking right back at me. My face was a smiling one. I had come here to have fun and learn even more Science.

It was soon time for the competition to start. We all sat around, holding our projects close to us. Even though this was the first time that I had participated in a competition (other than the farting contests with Damya), surprisingly I was not nervous at all. I had so enjoyed working on my Science project that the results did not matter in the least. Mr. Harish suggested leaving my solar cooker outside in the sun. The pot inside my solar cooker had been filled with water, and I had placed some rice inside it. Thankfully, it was a sweltering day. Even then it would require a few hours for the water to boil so the earlier I started, the better. My cooker then would have no problem in converting the sunshine to heat energy to cook the rice.

The competition had started. The name of the first participant was called out. It was a girl about my age, and she had a very interesting experiment to show. She gave everyone a piece of apple and a piece of potato. She then asked us all to hold our noses, close our eyes and then tell the difference between the two. I tried to do that and found that it was impossible to distinguish between the apple and the potato with the eyes and nose closed. She explained that since the nose and the mouth are connected through the same airway, we taste and smell food at the same time. Salty, sweet, bitter and sour tastes can be recognised by a sense of taste alone, but for some other tastes, you do need the sense of smell to recognise them as well. That is why it was difficult to distinguish the taste of the apple and the potato with eyes and nose closed. Fascinating! I loved participating in the experiment. I clapped loudly.

The second boy had an interesting experiment too. He had put four white coloured flowers in four different glasses. The glasses were filled with water. Some coloured ink had been mixed in each of the glasses. The first one had red ink; the second had black ink; the third had blue ink, and the fourth had green ink. What had happened eventually was that the petals of flowers had taken on the colour of the ink. So, the petals in the first glass had turned red; the second had turned black; the third had turned blue and the fourth green. This was because the water in the glass passes through the petal veins of the flower. So many new things to learn! It was all so very interesting.

One by one the children demonstrated their experiments. I clapped loudly for all of them. I was having such a fun time enjoying Science. It was almost afternoon by the time my turn came up.

I was now going to show them the rice that had been cooked simply by harnessing the energy of the sun. I went out and brought in my solar cooker with me. I explained the various parts of the solar cooker and the function of each. I then explained the Science behind each part. It was now time to open the pot to see whether the rice had been cooked by solar energy. I opened the pot slowly to find the rice merrily bubbling away. I heard an 'Aah' go around the room. My experiment had worked successfully. I had used the heat energy from the sunshine to cook rice in my very own solar cooker. I spent a few minutes explaining that the solar cooker had been invented a very long time ago by a Swiss inventor. This was just my re-creation. I went on to say that solar energy could also be used to supply power to villages like Rampur and Seetapur and I hoped that it would be used for the progress of villages. There were some people from the Government of India there. I could see it on their badges. Hearing how solar energy could be used for the progress of villages, they sat up and started taking notes furiously. There was also a person from the national newspaper there. He had been busy taking notes ever since the competition started.

When the results were announced, I was amongst the children who had won! The panel had been very impressed with my solar cooker. Mr. Harish gave me a hug. I was pleased and wished that I could celebrate with all the Rampurkars. However, that was not to be. My win would have to remain a secret because Science had been banned from the village of Rampur. I envied the celebrations that Seetapur was carrying out for children that had won from their village. They were celebrating Science while we could not. We did not have time to linger any further. We had to get back to our village.

Chapter Thirteen

Mr. Harish made it a point to get a copy of the national newspaper the next day from somewhere. When we saw it, we were stunned. The people from the Government of India and the newspaper man had certainly been busy. There were two major news items and both related to Rampur! The news items were as follows:

Headline One: Government of India astounded to hear about the ban on Science in Rampur

The Government of India is astounded to learn that Science has been banned in the tiny village of Rampur. After detailed investigations, carried out by our reporters, it was found that the ban was called by two powerful men in the village - the Sarpanch and the village holy Baba. The Government of India is deeply perturbed to hear this news especially since it is doing its best to promote Science in smaller villages like Rampur. So much that a Science teacher had also been sent to the village, albeit belatedly. It is this newspaper's view that the Sarpanch and the Baba are leading the villagers astray with their goofy superstitions, beliefs, and practices. The Rampurkars are being ruled by fear as people are going around threateningly with sickles in their hands if anyone dares to indulge in Science. This newspaper calls upon the people of India to revolt against such practices that are holding the country back…. Blah Blah Blah…...

Headline Two: Brave Jambhula wins one of the Seetapur Village Science Award

Jambhula, a girl from the village of Rampur which has made news for banning Science, has gone on to win an award at the annual children's Science competition that was held in the village of Seetapur. Jambhula deserves special mention because she dared to indulge in Science and attended the Science competition putting her little toe at serious risk. Rampur has recently enforced a new rule on its villagers wherein anyone found engaging in evil science (as they call it) would have their little toe chopped off. Our reporters further found out that if anyone with a missing little toe indulged in "evil" science, then they would have the other little toe chopped off. If they continued to engage in Science, then their little finger would go, followed by the next little finger and so on. This just goes to show what a brave thing Jambhula has done by attending the Science competition in such a hostile environment, all for the love of Science. It is the newspaper's view that children like Jambhula should be encouraged in their pursuit of Science. This newspaper calls on the people of India to shower praises on children like Jambhula and encourage her in her endeavour. Blah Blah Blah.

The other Rampurkars were flummoxed to learn that I had attended a Science competition secretly, risking my little toe in the process. The entire village collected besides the mango tree. Everybody was busy discussing the newspaper articles. Suddenly there was no fear in any of us. Our protests had worked! The people of India were on our side, and there was no reason to be afraid. People power had won. Several villagers came over to congratulate me. Damya had his mouth open in a wide 'O' when he saw me. Radha was pleased for me, and so were Santya, Ganya, Chiltya and all the others.

A very subdued looking Baba and Sarpanch stood in front of the people. Now that the Government of India had made their views clear, Baba and Sarpanch simply did not have the strength to fight. They were badly outnumbered not only by the Rampurkars but also the rest of the people in India. Group 4 reluctantly put their sickles down.

"The ban on Science has been revoked. You are now free to practice Science to your heart's content", was the announcement made by a restrained Sarpanch.

The crowd went crazy. They let out a whoop of delight and lifted Mr. Harish, his hair flying all over the place, on their shoulders. He would soon be standing as a Sarpanch for the next elections, and there was no doubt that he would win. Somebody got the dhol out, and everybody started to dance to the heady beats. Damya got left over gulal and soon all of us were as red as a beetroot, dancing madly and smiling widely.

Some villagers then came over and lifted me up high in the air too! People started cheering even more. They had probably forgotten already that I was a darky. Or maybe it did not really matter anymore. Mr. Harish had drilled it into our heads that all our internal organs were the same whether we liked it or not. Red blood, whitish green mucus, stinky farts, and smelly armpits – yup – no one could escape them, king or pauper.

The cheers continued for a long time. I thoroughly enjoyed it all. I would now be able to indulge in Science to my heart's desire.

Epilogue – Five years later

This has to be the most exciting day ever. The Prime

Minister of India is so impressed with the village that

she is personally going to pay us a visit. The

preparations started almost a month back. Hordes of

security people had arrived and scrutinised every

corner of our tiny village. There was so much noise, so much chaos and so much excitement in sleepy Rampur. The most thrilling part of all was the fact that the PM was personally going to hand over a certificate of achievement to me. Though I had won the Science competition almost five years ago, it was believed that it was on that memorable day that Rampur had taken a strong positive step towards Science.

A podium covered with the village flowers had been set up under the mango tree where the PM would make her speech. The PM was over two hours late but no one really minded. We had heard her cavalcade before we saw it. A series of white cars came in covering our village in dust. The PM's car was somewhere in the middle of all those cars. The PM went straight to the podium. Standing tall and looking very confident, she was dressed in a simple cream coloured sari. My ambitions soared just looking at her.

She was leading our country. What a woman! And what an honour to receive my certificate from her.

"Dear children of Rampur", she said in her clear, confident voice. A happy applause went around our village. She was going to make a speech addressing the children of Rampur.

"Firstly, I would like to personally apologise for forgetting to send a Science teacher to Rampur for so long. I ask your forgiveness with folded hands," she said. The crowd gave her another happy applause. Here was the PM apologising to us!

"It is unbelievable how much your village has achieved in this short span of time. I am very impressed indeed". Another applause.

"Science had always been one of my favourite subjects in school. I believe that our country can make tremendous progress if all of us take a greater interest in Science. I am trying to encourage other villages to follow the example of Rampur. The children of Rampur have set an example for others".

Then she continued more quietly.

"I believe, that there is one particular girl, who decided to participate in a Science competition even when her little toe was at risk. It is this girl that I want to honour today. Our country will progress in no time if we have feisty children like her".

Everyone turned to look at me. I gave them all my brightest smile. This was my moment, and I was going to enjoy it to the full.

"Can Jambhula, please come to the podium?"

I walked up. While the PM's aides scrambled about to get the certificate out, the PM stood with her hand on my shoulder.

"Here's to the future," she said. Everyone was madly clapping now. Somewhere in the crowd, I saw Baba's and Amma's gratified face. They were probably crying, but I wasn't too sure. Damya was clapping wildly, jumping all over the place. Even the Baba and Sarpanch were clapping with wide grins on their faces.

I took the certificate from the PM and held it securely. From now on, this was going to be my most treasured possession. The PM looked at me and gave me a tiny wink! Oh, how much I wanted to be like her.

The PM then got down to all the serious stuff. A fund to help with the scientific progress was announced. It was clear that the Prime Minister of India was in a very good mood indeed.

"I now declare Rampur as the 'Village of Science', shouted the PM making full use of her healthy lungs. The clapping started and did not die down for fifteen minutes.

Rampur had changed in so many ways since the day that I had won the Science competition. Mr. Harish has become the Sarpanch of the village. He had easily got most the votes. He made an excellent Sarpanch guiding the village towards scientific progress. The village has started to attract several more Science teachers for not only for the children but adults too. All the villagers including the Baba and the ex-Sarpanch now take a keen interest in Science. Group 4 and other members of the Gram Panchayat are slowly coming around too. Mr. Harish had consistently explained the benefits of Science to them, and since they were now being outnumbered, they had decided to join the Science gang.

The village now has a tiny hospital headed by Doctor Sahab. The reputation of being a village of Science has spread far and wide, and several doctors have made their way to work in the village. Several complicated surgeries are now performed in the village itself.

The villagers frequently conduct their own experiments with the result that the village has plenty of new inventions and innovations. Ramdev is working on a scientific belt which when worn would allow him to become invisible. He has had several failed attempts but is determined, and so he perseveres. Rambhau is working on the herb that would help control stinky farts. Seetabai is working on a cap which when worn would allow her to read the minds of people. Keshavnath is working on a pill which when consumed would turn grey hair to a darker shade for ever after. Leela bai is working on a rocket that would launch faster than any of the current ones. Mr. Harish himself is working on a concoction to tame his wild and frizzy hair. I am waiting for Mr. Harish's concoction to succeed so that I can use it to control my hair too. Amma no longer fears Science but now takes an active interest in it.

Through the efforts of these scientific villagers, Rampur is now powered by a solar grid. We now have light in our lives. We can get hot water whenever we want. All the families have solar cookers. I can see my tiny project taking shape before my eyes, and it is totally unbelievable. All villagers have access to compost toilets which have been placed in semi-solid structures outside the house as we Rampurkars are still reluctant to have a poo-room INSIDE our huts. Being

educated about the dangers of poo-ing in the open, we

were slowly becoming convinced that we would have

to get used to using toilets. I had to break the solemn

pledge that I had made about not pooing inside a room.

I am now utterly convinced of the scientific benefits of

pooing inside a toilet, and I took to the toilets in no

time at all.

Perhaps the most important change was in the

attitude of the villagers. Rampurkars have finally let go

of their prejudices and superstitious beliefs. We no

longer believe that burping or farting twice can solve a

problem or that somersaulting thrice will cause

runaway cows to come back. Damya, the other darkies

and I, are now allowed in the temple just like everyone

else. The villagers do not fear ghosts, witches or evil

eyes. We play under the supposedly haunted Peepal

tree all the time, even at night. Darkies and the fair

167

ones have started collaborating on Science projects. They even eat together. Girls are now encouraged to succeed. Kala's daughter has become a school teacher – a dream that she had had since childhood. There are so many discoveries to be made, so much more to innovate. No one can resist the power of Science. Science has won!

Mr. Harish is guiding and encouraging my journey to become a scientist. I want to become as confident as the PM herself. Everything and everyone are changing. Damya though has remained his usual self.

Glossary

Adda - meeting place

Aiyyo – an exclamation exclusive to India

Amla - Indian gooseberry

Amma - mother

Baba - father; religious men, are often referred to as babas.

Bapu - father

Dhol - drums

Dhoti - a traditional piece of clothing that is worn in India by the men in place of trousers.

Diya – traditional Indian lamp

Gram panchayat - a village council

Gulal - red colour

Jambhul - a fruit also known as Jamun in Hindi or Java plum, Black plum and Indian blackberry in English

Laddu - an Indian sweet

Peepal - a tree found in the Indian subcontinent

Sadhu - religious person

Sahab - a term of respect

Sarpanch - an elected leader of the gram panchayat of a village